KU-574-651

Little Old Mrs Pepperpot

Things are pretty difficult for Mrs Pepperpot – she is never sure if she is going to be her normal size, or tiny like a pepperpot. How can she go and see her friends, get the supper cooked, and stop the cat from thinking she is a mouse? And what will be her fate when she gets stuck in a drawer of macaroni at the grocers?

Mrs Pepperpot's hilarious adventures as she copes with these difficulties will have you in stitches.

Alf Prøysen was born in Norway, and has written stories (including other *Mrs Pepperpot* stories) and poems for children, a weekly newspaper column and a series of programmes for radio.

ALF PRØYSEN
Little Old Mrs Pepperpot

Illustrated by Bjorn Berg

Beaver Books

A Beaver Book

Published by Arrow Books Limited
Brookmount House, 62-65 Chandos Place,
Covent Garden, London, WC2N 4NW

A division of the Hutchinson Publishing Group
London Melbourne Sydney Auckland Johannesburg
and agencies throughout the world

First published by Hutchinson Junior Books 1959
Beaver edition 1984
Reprint 1985

© Copyright text Alf Prøysen 1960
© Copyright English translation Hutchinson 1959

This book is sold subject to the condition that it
shall not, by way of trade or otherwise, be lent,
resold, hired out, or otherwise circulated without the publisher's prior consent in any form of
binding or cover other than that in which it is
published and without a similar condition including this condition being imposed on the
subsequent purchaser

**Made and printed in Great Britain by the
Guernsey Press Co. Ltd., Guernsey, Channel Islands**

ISBN 0 09 938050 1

Contents

Little old Mrs. Pepperpot

THERE was once an old woman who went to bed at night as old women usually do, and in the morning she woke up as old women usually do. But on this particular morning she found herself shrunk to the size of a pepperpot, and old women don't usually do that. The odd thing was, her name really was Mrs. Pepperpot.

'Well, as I'm now the size of a pepperpot, I shall have to make the best of it,' she said to herself, for she had no one else to talk to; her husband was out in the fields and all her children were grown up and gone away.

Now she happened to have a great deal to do that day. First of all she had to clean the house, then there was all the washing which was lying in soak and waiting to be done, and lastly she had to make pancakes for supper.

'I must get out of bed somehow,' she thought, and, taking hold of a corner of the eiderdown, she started rolling herself up in it. She rolled and rolled until the eiderdown was like a huge sausage, which fell softly on the floor. Mrs. Pepperpot crawled out and she hadn't hurt herself a bit.

The first job was to clean the house, but that was quite easy; she just sat down in front of a mouse-hole and squeaked till the mouse came out.

'Clean the house from top to bottom,' she said, 'or I'll tell the cat about you.' So the mouse cleaned the house from top to bottom.

Mrs. Pepperpot called the cat: 'Puss! Puss! Lick out all the plates and dishes or I'll tell the dog about you.' And the cat licked all the plates and dishes clean.

Then the old woman called the dog. 'Listen, dog; you make the bed and open the window and I'll give you a bone as a reward.' So the dog did as he was told, and when he had finished he sat down on the front door-step and waved his tail so hard he made the step shine like a mirror.

'You'll have to get the bone yourself,' said Mrs. Pepperpot, 'I haven't time to wait on people.' She pointed to the window-sill where a large bone lay.

After this she wanted to start her washing. She had put it to soak in the brook, but the brook was almost dry. So she sat down and started muttering in a discontented sort of way:

'I have lived a long time, but in all my born days I never saw the brook so dry. If we don't have a shower soon, I expect everyone will die of thirst.' Over and over again she said it, all the time looking up at the sky.

At last the raincloud in the sky got so angry that it decided to drown the old woman altogether. But she crawled under a monk's-hood flower, where she stayed snug and warm while the rain poured down and rinsed her clothes clean in the brook.

Now the old woman started muttering again: 'I have lived a long time, but in all my born days I have never known such a feeble South Wind as we have had lately. I'm sure if the South Wind started blowing this minute it couldn't lift me off the ground, even though I am no bigger than a pepperpot.'

The South Wind heard this and instantly came tearing along, but Mrs. Pepperpot hid in an empty badger set, and from there she watched the South Wind blow all the clothes right up on to her clothes-line.

Again she started muttering: 'I have lived a long time, but in all my born days I have never seen the sun give so little heat in the middle of the summer. It seems to have lost all its power, that's a fact.'

When the sun heard this it turned scarlet with rage and sent down fiery rays to give the old woman sunstroke. But by this time she was safely back in her house, and was sailing about the sink in a saucer. Meanwhile the furious sun dried all the clothes on the line.

'Now for cooking the supper,' said Mrs. Pepperpot; 'my husband will be back in an hour and, by hook or by crook, thirty pancakes must be ready on the table.'

She had mixed the dough for the pancakes in a bowl the day before. Now she sat down beside the bowl and said: 'I have always been fond of you, bowl, and I've told all the neighbours that there's not a bowl like you anywhere. I am sure, if you really wanted to, you could walk straight over to the cooking-stove and turn it on.'

And the bowl went straight over to the stove and turned it on.

Then Mrs. Pepperpot said: 'I'll never forget the day I bought my frying-pan. There were lots of pans in the shop, but I said: "If I can't have that pan hanging right over the shop assistant's head, I won't buy any pan at all. For that is the best pan in the whole world, and I'm sure if I were ever in trouble that pan could jump on to the stove by itself." '

And there and then the frying-pan jumped on to the stove. And when it was hot enough, the bowl tilted itself to let the dough run on to the pan.

Then the old woman said: 'I once read a fairy-tale about a pancake which could roll along the road. It was the stupidest story that ever I read. But I'm sure the pancake on the pan could easily turn a somersault in the air if it really wanted to.'

At this the pancake took a great leap from sheer pride and turned a somersault as Mrs. Pepperpot had said. Not only one pancake, but *all* the pancakes did this, and the bowl went on tilting and the pan went on frying until, before the hour was up, there were thirty pancakes on the dish.

Then Mr. Pepperpot came home. And, just as he opened the door, Mrs. Pepperpot turned back to her usual size. So they sat down and ate their supper.

And the old woman said nothing about having been as small as a pepperpot, because old women don't usually talk about such things.

Mrs. Pepperpot and the mechanical doll

IT WAS two days before Christmas. Mrs. Pepperpot hummed and sang as she trotted round her kitchen, she was so pleased to be finished with all her Christmas preparations. The pig had been killed, the sausages made, and now all she had to do was to brew herself a cup of coffee and sit down for a little rest.

'How lovely that Christmas is here,' she said, 'then everybody's happy—especially the children—that's the best of all; to see them happy and well.'

The old woman was almost like a child herself because of this knack she had of suddenly shrinking to the size of a pepperpot.

She was thinking about all this while she was making her coffee, and she had just poured it into the cup when there was a knock at the door.

'Come in,' she said, and in came a little girl who was oh! so pale and thin.

'Poor child! Wherever do you live—I'm sure I've never seen you before,' said Mrs. Pepperpot.

'I'm Hannah. I live in the little cottage at the edge of

16

the forest,' said the child, 'and I'm just going round to all the houses to ask if anybody has any old Christmas decorations left over from last year—glitter or paper-chains or glass balls or anything, you know. Have *you* got anything you don't need?'

'I expect so, Hannah,' answered Mrs. Pepperpot, and went up into the attic to fetch the cardboard box with all the decorations. She gave it to the little girl.

'How lovely! Can I really have all that?'

'You can,' said Mrs. Pepperpot, 'and you shall have something else as well. Tomorrow I will bring you a big doll.'

'I don't believe that,' said Hannah.

'Why not?'

'You haven't *got* a doll.'

'That's simple; I'll buy one,' said Mrs. Pepperpot. 'I'll bring it over tomorrow afternoon, but I must be home by six o'clock because it's Christmas Eve.'

'How wonderful if you can come tomorrow afternoon—I shall be all alone. Father and Mother both go out to work, you see, and they don't get back until the church bells have rung.'

So the little girl went home, and Mrs. Pepperpot went down to the toy-shop and bought a big doll. But when she woke up next morning there she was, once more, no bigger than a pepperpot.

'How provoking!' she said to herself. 'On this day of all days, when I have to take the doll to Hannah. Never mind! I expect I'll manage.'

After she had dressed she tried to pick up the doll, but it was much too heavy for her to lift.

'I'll have to go without it,' she thought, and opened the door to set off.

But oh dear! it had been snowing hard all night, and the little old woman soon sank deep in the snowdrifts. The cat was sitting in front of the house; when she saw something moving in the snow she thought it was a mouse and jumped on it.

'Hi, stop!' shouted Mrs. Pepperpot. 'Keep your claws to yourself! Can't you see it's just me shrunk again?'

'I beg your pardon,' said the cat, and started walking away.

'Wait a minute,' said Mrs. Pepperpot, 'to make up for your mistake you can give me a ride down to the main road.' The cat was quite willing, so she lay down and let the little old woman climb on her back. When they got to the main road the cat stopped. 'Can you hear anything?' asked Mrs. Pepperpot.

'Yes, I think it's the snow-plough,' said the cat, 'so we'll have to get out of the way, or we'll be buried in snow.'

'I don't want to get out of the way,' said Mrs. Pepperpot, and she sat down in the middle of the road and waited till the snow-plough was right in front of her; then she jumped up and landed smack on the front tip of the plough.

There she sat, clinging on for dear life and enjoying herself hugely. 'Look at me, the little old woman, driving the snow-plough!' she laughed.

When the snow-plough had almost reached the door of Hannah's little cottage, she climbed on to the edge nearest the side of the road and, before you could say Jack Robinson, she had landed safely on the great mound of snow thrown up by the plough. From there she could walk right across Hannah's hedge and slide down the other side. She was shaking the snow off her clothes on the doorstep when Hannah came out and picked her up.

'Are you one of those mechanical dolls that you wind up?' asked Hannah.

'No,' said Mrs. Pepperpot, 'I am a woman who can wind myself up, thank you very much. Help me brush off all the snow and then let's go inside.'

'Are you perhaps the old woman who shrinks to the size of a pepperpot?'

'Of course I am, silly.'

'Where's the doll you were going to bring me?' asked Hannah when they got inside.

'I've got it at home. You'll have to go back with me and fetch it. It's too heavy for me.'

'Shouldn't you have something to eat, now that you've come to see me? Would you like a biscuit?' And the little girl held out a biscuit in the shape of a ring.

'Thank you very much,' said Mrs. Pepperpot and popped her head through the biscuit ring.

Oh, how the little girl laughed! 'I quite forgot you were so small,' she said; 'let me break it into little pieces so that you can eat it.' Then she fetched a thimble and filled it with fruit juice. 'Have a drink,' she said.

'Thank you,' said Mrs. Pepperpot.

After that they played a lot of good games; ride-a-cock-horse with Mrs. Pepperpot sitting on Hannah's knee, and hide-and-seek. But the little girl had an awful time trying to find Mrs. Pepperpot—she hid in such awkward places. When they had finished playing Hannah put on her coat and with Mrs. Pepperpot in her pocket she went off to fetch her beautiful big doll.

'Oh, thank you!' she exclaimed when she saw it. 'But do you know,' she added, 'I would really rather have *you* to play with all the time.'

'You can come and see me again if you like,' said Mrs. Pepperpot, 'I am often as small as a pepperpot, and then it's nice to have a little help around the house. And, of course, we can play games as well.'

So now the little girl often spends her time with **Mrs.**
Pepperpot. She looks ever so much better, and they
often talk about the day Mrs. Pepperpot arrived on the
snow-plough, and about the doll she gave Hannah.

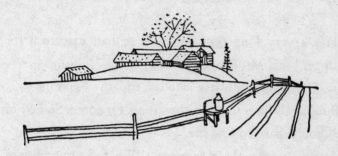

Mr. Pepperpot buys macaroni

'IT's a very long time since we've had macaroni for supper,' said Mr. Pepperpot one day.

'Then you shall have it today, my love,' said his wife. 'But I shall have to go to the grocer for some. So first of all you'll have to find me.'

'Find you?' said Mr. Pepperpot. 'What sort of nonsense is that?' But when he looked round for her he couldn't see her anywhere. 'Don't be silly, wife,' he said; 'if you're hiding in the cupboard you must come out this minute. We're too big to play hide-and-seek.'

'I'm not too big, I'm just the right size for "hunt-the-pepperpot",' laughed Mrs. Pepperpot. 'Find me if you can!'

'I'm not going to charge round my own bedroom looking for my wife,' he said crossly.

'Now, now! I'll help you; I'll tell you when you're warm. Just now you're very cold.' For Mr. Pepperpot was peering out of the window, thinking she might have jumped out. As he searched round the room she called out 'Warm!', 'Colder!', 'Getting hotter!' until he was quite dizzy.

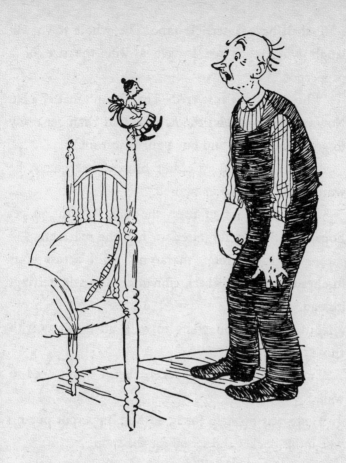

At last she shouted, 'You'll burn the top of your bald head if you don't look up!' And there she was, sitting on the bedpost, swinging her legs and laughing at him.

Her husband pulled a very long face when he saw her. 'This is a bad business—a very bad business,' he said, stroking her cheek with his little finger.

'I don't think it's a bad business,' said Mrs. Pepperpot.

'I shall have a terrible time. The whole town will laugh when they see I have a wife the size of a pepperpot.'

'Who cares?' she answered. 'That doesn't matter a bit. Now put me down on the floor so that I can get ready to go to the grocer and buy your macaroni.'

But her husband wouldn't hear of her going; he would go to the grocer himself.

'That'll be a lot of use!' she said. 'When you get home you'll have forgotten to buy the macaroni. I'm sure even if I wrote "macaroni" right across your forehead you'd bring back cinnamon and salt herrings instead.'

'But how are you going to walk all that way with those tiny legs?'

'Put me in your coat pocket; then I won't need to walk.'

There was no help for it, so Mr. Pepperpot put his wife in his pocket and set off for the shop.

Soon she started talking: "My goodness me, what a lot of strange things you have in your pocket—screws and nails, tobacco and matches—there's even a fish-hook! You'll have to take that out at once; I might get it caught in my skirt.'

'Don't talk so loud,' said her husband as he took out the fish-hook. 'We're going into the shop now.'

It was an old-fashioned village store where they sold everything from prunes to coffee cups. The grocer was particularly proud of the coffee cups and held one up for Mr. Pepperpot to see. This made his wife curious and she popped her head out of his pocket.

'You stay where you are!' whispered Mr. Pepperpot.

'I beg your pardon, did you say anything?' asked the grocer.

'No, no, I was just humming a little tune,' said Mr. Pepperpot. 'Tra-la-la!'

'What colour are the cups?' whispered his wife. And her husband sang:

> 'The cups are blue
> With gold edge too,
> But they cost too much
> So that won't do!'

After that Mrs. Pepperpot kept quiet—but not for long. When her husband pulled out his tobacco tin she couldn't resist hanging on to the lid. Neither her husband nor anyone else in the shop noticed her slipping on to the counter and hiding behind a flour-bag. From there she darted silently across to the scales, crawled under them, past a pair of kippers wrapped in newspaper, and found herself next to the coffee cups.

'Aren't they pretty!' she whispered, and took a step backwards to get a better view. Whoops! She fell right into the macaroni drawer which had been left open. She hastily covered herself up with macaroni, but the grocer heard the scratching noise and quickly banged the drawer shut. You see, it did sometimes happen that mice got in the drawers, and that's not the sort of thing you want people to know about, so the grocer pretended nothing had happened and went on serving.

There was Mrs. Pepperpot all in the dark; she could hear the grocer serving her husband now. 'That's good,' she thought. 'When he orders macaroni I'll get my chance to slip into the bag with it.'

But it was just as she had feared; her husband forgot what he had come to buy. Mrs. Pepperpot shouted at the top of her voice, 'MACARONI!', but it was impossible to get him to hear.

'A quarter of a pound of coffee, please,' said her husband.

'Anything else?' asked the grocer.

'MACARONI!' shouted Mrs. Pepperpot.

'Two pounds of sugar,' said her husband.

'Anything more?'

'MACARONI!' shouted Mrs. Pepperpot.

But at last her husband remembered the macaroni of his own accord. The grocer hurriedly filled a bag. He thought he felt something move, but he didn't say a word.

'That's all, thank you,' said Mr. Pepperpot. When he got outside the door he was just about to make sure his

wife was still in his pocket when a van drew up and offered to give him a lift all the way home. Once there he took off his knapsack with all the shopping in it and put his hand in his pocket to lift out his wife.

The pocket was empty.

Now he was really frightened. First he thought she was teasing him, but when he had called three times and still no wife appeared, he put on his hat again and hurried back to the shop.

The grocer saw him coming. 'He's probably going to complain about the mouse in the macaroni,' he thought.

'Have you forgotten anything, Mr. Pepperpot?' he asked, and smiled as pleasantly as he could.

Mr. Pepperpot was looking all round. 'Yes,' he said.

'I would be very grateful, Mr. Pepperpot, if you would keep it to yourself about the mouse being in the macaroni. I'll let you have these fine blue coffee cups if you'll say no more about it.'

'Mouse?' Mr. Pepperpot looked puzzled.

'Shh!' said the grocer, and hurriedly started wrapping up the cups.

Then Mr. Pepperpot realized that the grocer had mistaken his wife for a mouse. So he took the cups and rushed home as fast as he could. By the time he got there he was in a sweat of fear that his wife might have been squeezed to death in the macaroni bag.

'Oh, my dear wife,' he muttered to himself. 'My poor darling wife. I'll never again be ashamed of you being the size of a pepperpot—as long as you're still alive!'

When he opened the door she was standing by the cooking-stove, dishing up the macaroni—as large as life; in fact, as large as you or I.

Queen of the Crows

DID you know that the woman who was as small as a pepperpot was queen of all the crows in the forest?

No, of course you didn't, because it was a secret between Mrs. Pepperpot and me until now. But now I'm going to tell you how it happened.

Outside the old woman's house there was a wooden fence and on it used to sit a large crow.

'I can't understand why that crow has to sit there staring in at the kitchen window all the time,' said Mr. Pepperpot.

'I can't imagine,' said Mrs. Pepperpot. 'Shoo! Get along with you!'

But the crow didn't move from the fence.

Then one day Mrs. Pepperpot had her shrinking turn again (I can't remember now what she was supposed to be doing that day, but she was very busy), and by the time she had clambered over the doorstep she was quite out of breath.

'Oh dear, it's certainly hard to be so small,' she puffed.

Suddenly there was a sound of flapping wings and the

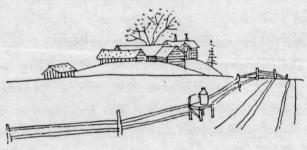

crow swooped down, picked up Mrs. Pepperpot by her skirt and flew up over the highest fir trees in the forest with her.

'What's the idea, may I ask? You wait till I'm back to my proper size and I'll beat you with my birch rod and chase you off for good!'

'Caw-caw! You're small enough now, at any rate,' said the crow; 'I've waited a long time for this. I saw you turn small once before, you see, so I thought it might happen again. And here we are, but only just in time. Today is the Crows' Festival and *I'm* to be Queen of the Crows!'

'If you're to be Queen of the Crows, you surely don't need to take an old woman like me along?'

'That's just where you're wrong,' said the crow, and flapped her wings; the old woman was heavier than she had expected. 'Wait till we get back to my nest, then you'll see why.'

'There's not much else I *can* do,' thought poor Mrs. Pepperpot as she dangled from the crow's claws.

'Here we are; home!' said the crow, and dropped Mrs. Pepperpot into the nest. 'Lucky it's empty.'

'It certainly is; I fell right on a spiky twig and grazed my shinbone.'

'Poor little thing!' said the crow. 'But look, I've made you a lovely bed of feathers and down. You'll find the down very snug and warm, and the feathers are just the thing when night falls and the wind begins to blow.'

'What do I want with feathers and down?'

'I want you to lie down and go to sleep,' said the crow. 'But first you must lend me your clothes. So please take off your head-scarf now, and your blouse and your skirt.

'The scarf I want you to tie round my neck, the skirt goes on one wing and the blouse on the other. Then I shall fly to the clearing in the forest where all the crows are meeting for the Festival. The finest-looking crow will be chosen queen, and that's going to be me! When I win I'll think of you. Caw-caw!'

'Well, if you think you'll be any better looking in my old clothes, you're welcome,' said Mrs. Pepperpot as she dressed up the crow.

'Hurry, hurry!' said the crow. 'There's another crow living over there in that fir tree on the hill. She'll be dropping in here on her way; we were going to the Festival together. But now that I'm all dressed up I'd rather go alone. Caw-caw-caw!' And off she flew.

Mrs. Pepperpot sat shivering in her petticoat, but then she thought of burrowing deep under the feathers and down as the crow had told her to do, and she found she was soon warm and cosy.

Suddenly the whole branch started swaying, and on the end perched a huge crow.

'Mary Crow, are you at home?' croaked the crow, sidling up and poking her big beak over the edge of the nest.

'Mary Crow has gone to the Festival,' said Mrs. Pepperpot.

'Then who are you, who are you?' asked the crow.

'I'm just an old woman shivering with cold, because Mary Crow has borrowed my clothes.'

'Caw-caw! Oh blow! She'll be the finest-looking crow at the Festival,' shrieked the crow as she threw herself into the air from the branch. 'But I'll have the scarf off her!'

Mrs. Pepperpot lay down to sleep again. Suddenly she rolled right over into the corner of the nest, the branch was shaking so much.

'That'll be another crow,' she thought, and quite right, it was; the biggest crow she had ever seen was swinging on the tip of the branch.

'Mary Crow, Mary Crow, have you seen Betty Crow?'

'I've seen both Mary Crow *and* Betty Crow,' said Mrs. Pepperpot.

'Who are you, who are you?' squawked the crow.

'I'm just an old woman shivering with cold because Mary Crow has borrowed my clothes.'

'Caw-caw! What a bore! Now Mary Crow will be the best-looking crow.'

'I'm not so sure about that,' said the old woman, 'because Betty Crow flew after Mary Crow and was going to have the scarf off her.'

'I'll take the skirt, I'll take the skirt!' croaked the biggest crow, and took off from the branch with such a bound that Mrs. Pepperpot had to hold on tight not to get thrown out of the nest.

In the clearing in the forest there were lots and lots of crows. They sat round in a circle and, one by one, they hopped into the middle to show themselves. Some of the crows could hop on one leg without touching the ground with their wings. Others had different kinds of tricks, and the crows sitting round had to choose the best one to be their queen.

At last there were only three crows left. They sat well away from each other, polishing their feathers and looking very fierce indeed. One had a scarf, the second had a skirt and the third had a blouse. So you can guess which crows *they* were. One of them was to be chosen queen.

'The crow with the scarf round her neck is the best,' said some of the crows, 'she looks most like a human being.'

'No, no; the crow with the skirt looks best!'

'Not at all! The crow with the blouse looks most dignified, and a queen should be dignified.'

Suddenly something fell with a bump to the ground; the jay had arrived right in the middle of the Festival with a strange-looking bird in its beak.

'Caw-caw! The jay has no business to be here!' croaked all the crows.

'I won't stay a minute,' said the jay. 'I've just brought you your queen!' and he flew off.

All the crows stared at the strange little raggedy bird in the middle of the ring. They could see it was covered in crow's feathers and down, but raggedy crows could not be allowed at the Festival.

'It's against the law!' said the biggest crow.

'Let's peck it, let's peck it!' said Mary Crow.

'Yes, let's hack it to pieces!' said Betty Crow.

'Yes, yes!' croaked all the crows. 'We can't have raggedy birds here!'

'Wait a minute!' said the raggedy bird, and climbed on to a tree-stump. 'I'll sing you a song.' And before they could stop it, it started singing 'Who Killed Cock Robin?' And it knew all the verses. The crows were delighted; they clapped and flapped their wings till the raggedy bird lost nearly all its feathers.

'D'you know any more? D'you know any more?' they croaked.

'I can dance the polka,' said the raggedy bird, and danced round the circle till they were all out of breath.

'You shall be our Queen!' they all shouted. 'Four Court Crows will carry you wherever you wish to go.'

'How wonderful!' laughed the Queen of the Crows. 'Then they must carry me to the house over there by the edge of the forest.'

'What would Your Majesty like to wear?'

'I would like to wear a skirt, a blouse and a head-scarf,' said the Queen.

Much later that night there was a knock at the cottage door. Mr. Pepperpot opened it, and there stood his wife.

'You're very late, wife,' he said. 'Where have you been?'

'I've been to a Festival,' she answered.

'But why are you covered in feathers?'

'You just go to bed and don't trouble yourself,' said Mrs. Pepperpot. She went over and stuck a feather in the corner of the window.

'Why do you do that?' asked her husband.

'For no reason at all.'

But she really did it because she had been chosen Queen of the Crows.

Mrs. Pepperpot at the bazaar

ONE day Mrs. Pepperpot was alone in her kitchen. At least, she was not *quite* alone, because Hannah, the little girl who had had the doll for Christmas, was there as well. She was busy scraping out a bowl and licking the spoon, for the old woman had been making gingerbread shapes.

There was a knock at the door. Mrs. Pepperpot said, 'Come in.' And in walked three very smart ladies.

'Good afternoon,' said the smart ladies. 'We are collecting prizes for the lottery at the school bazaar this evening. Do you think you have some little thing we could have? The money from the bazaar is for the boys' brass band—they need new instruments.'

'Oh, I'd like to help with that,' said Mrs. Pepperpot, for she dearly loved brass bands. 'Would a plate of gingerbread be any use?'

'Of course,' said the smart ladies, but they laughed behind her back. 'We could take it with us now if you have it ready,' they said. But Mrs. Pepperpot wanted to go to the bazaar herself, so she said she would bring the gingerbread.

So the three smart ladies went away and Mrs. Pepperpot was very proud and pleased that she was going to a bazaar.

Hannah was still scraping away at the bowl and licking the sweet mixture from the spoon.

'May I come with you?' she asked.

'Certainly, if your father and mother will let you.'

'I'm sure they will,' said the child, 'because Father has to work at the factory and Mother is at her sewing all day.'

'Be here at six o'clock then,' said Mrs. Pepperpot, and started making another batch of gingerbread shapes.

But when Hannah came back at six the old woman was not there. All the doors were open, so she went from room to room, calling her. When she got back to the kitchen she heard an odd noise coming from the table. The mixing bowl was upside down, so she lifted it carefully. And there underneath sat her friend who was now again as small as a pepperpot.

'Isn't this a nuisance?' said Mrs. Pepperpot. 'I was just cleaning out the bowl after putting the gingerbread in the oven when I suddenly started shrinking. Then the bowl turned over on me. Quick! Get the cakes out of the oven before they burn!'

But it was too late; the gingerbread was burnt to a cinder.

Mrs. Pepperpot sat down and cried, she was so disappointed. But she soon gave that up and started thinking instead. Suddenly she laughed out loud and said:

'Hannah! Put me under the tap and give me a good wash. We're going to the bazaar, you and I!'

'But you can't go to the bazaar like that!' said Hannah.

'Oh yes, I can,' said Mrs. Pepperpot, 'as long as you do what I say.'

Hannah promised, but Mrs. Pepperpot gave her some very queer orders. First she was to fetch a silk ribbon and tie it round the old woman so that it looked like a skirt. Then she was to fetch some tinsel from the Christmas decorations. This she had to wind round and round to make a silver bodice. And lastly she had to make a bonnet of gold foil.

'Now you must wrap me carefully in cellophane and put me in a cardboard box,' said Mrs. Pepperpot.

'Why?' asked Hannah.

'When I've promised them a prize for the bazaar they must have it,' said Mrs. Pepperpot, 'so I'm giving them myself. Just put me down on one of the tables and say you've brought a mechanical doll. Tell them you keep the key in your pocket and then pretend to wind me up so that people can see how clever I am.'

Hannah did as she was told, and when she got to the

bazaar and put the wonderful doll on the table, many people clapped their hands and crowded round to see.

'What a pretty doll!' they said. 'And what a lovely dress!'

'Look at her gold bonnet!'

Mrs. Pepperpot lay absolutely still in her cardboard box, but when she heard how everybody praised her, she winked at Hannah with one eye, and Hannah knew what she wanted. She lifted Mrs. Pepperpot very carefully out of the box and pretended to wind her up at the back with a key.

Everyone was watching her. But when Mrs. Pepperpot began walking across the table, picking her way through the prizes, there was great excitement.

'Look, the doll can walk!'

And when Mrs. Pepperpot began to dance they started shouting and yelling with delight, 'The doll is dancing!'

The three smart ladies who had been to see Mrs. Pepperpot earlier in the day sat in special seats and looked very grand. One of them had given six expensive coffee cups, the second an elegant table mat and the third a beautiful iced layer cake.

Mrs. Pepperpot decided to go over and speak to them, for she was afraid they had recognized her and thought it queer that she hadn't brought the gingerbread.

The three smart ladies were very pleased when the doll came walking across the table to them.

'Come to me!' said the one who had given the coffee cups, and stretched her hand out towards Mrs. Pepperpot, who walked on to it obediently.

'Let me hold her a little,' said the lady with the elegant table mat, and Mrs. Pepperpot went over to her hand.

'Now it's my turn,' said the lady with the iced cake.

'I'm sure they know it's me,' thought Mrs. Pepperpot, 'that's why they stare at me so hard and hold me on their hands.'

But then the lady with the cake said, 'Well, I must say, this is a much better prize than the gingerbread that the odd old woman offered us today.'

Now she should never have said that; Mrs. Pepperpot leaped straight out of her hand and landed PLOP! right in the middle of the beautiful iced layer cake. Then she got up and waded right through it. The cake lady screamed, but people were shouting with laughter by now.

'Take that doll away!' shrieked the second lady, but *squish, squash!* went Mrs. Pepperpot's sticky feet, right across her lovely table mat.

'Get that dreadful doll away!' cried the third lady. But it was too late; Mrs. Pepperpot was on the tray with

the expensive coffee cups, and began to dance a jig. Cups and saucers flew about and broke in little pieces.

What a-to-do! The conductor of the brass band had quite a job to quieten them all down. He announced that the winning numbers of the lottery would be given out.

'First prize will be the wonderful mechanical doll,' he said.

When Hannah heard that she was very frightened. What would happen if somebody won Mrs. Pepperpot, so that she couldn't go home to her husband? She tugged at Mrs. Pepperpot's skirt and whispered, 'Shall I put you in my pocket and creep away?'

'No,' said Mrs. Pepperpot.

'But think how awful it would be if someone won you and took you home.'

'What must be must be!' said Mrs. Pepperpot.

The conductor called out the winning number, '311!' Everyone looked at their tickets, but no one had number 311.

'That's a good thing!' sighed Hannah with relief. There would have to be another draw. But just then she remembered she had a ticket in her hand; it was number 311!

'Wait!' she cried, and showed her ticket. The conductor looked at it and saw it was the right one.

So Hannah was allowed to take Mrs. Pepperpot home.

Next day the old woman was her proper size again and Hannah only a little girl, and Mrs. Pepperpot said, 'You're my little girl, aren't you?'

'Yes,' said Hannah, 'and you're my very own Mrs. Pepperpot, because I won you at the bazaar yesterday.'

And that was the end of Mrs. Pepperpot's adventures for a very long time.

Mr. Puffblow's hat

THERE was once a man called Mr. Puffblow who had an enormous hat. Mr. Puffblow was a very severe sort of man, and when he walked down the street he used to get very angry indeed if any of the children stared at his hat. And if they as much as stopped and looked at the house where he lived he would rush out and chase them off, because he thought they wanted to steal his apples.

Nobody dared go against Mr. Puffblow. 'Ssh!' mothers would say to their children playing in the street. 'You'd better be quiet—Mr. Puffblow is coming this way!'

Every day at precisely half past eleven Mr. Puffblow walked down the street to fetch his pint of milk from the dairy. So, until *that* was over, everybody stayed indoors.

One day the West Wind came tearing through the town, and I don't think there is anything like the West Wind for upsetting things in the autumn; the mischief it gets up to is nobody's business.

Now suddenly the West Wind caught sight of Mr.

Puffblow walking down the street with his enormous hat on.

'Wheee!' said the West Wind. 'That's just the hat for me!'

So, with a puff and a blow, it tipped Mr. Puffblow's hat off his head.

The hat bowled along the pavement. Mr. Puffblow ran after it. But just as he was about to catch it, the West Wind pounced and blew it further away. This game went on for a long time until at last the West Wind carried the hat high up into the air, right over the rooftops of the town to the wood beyond.

'I'm tired of playing with you now,' said the West

Wind to the hat. 'I'm going to drop you in this brook and leave you to sink or swim. Good luck!'

The hat turned two more somersaults in the air, then plopped into the brook and floated away like a little round ship.

It so happened that a tiny fieldmouse had been out in the wood that day gathering nuts, and he had fallen into the brook. He could swim all right, but the current was so strong he was almost drowned struggling against it.

When he saw the hat sailing past he caught hold of the brim with his paws and clambered up to the top of the crown.

'This would make a very good ship,' thought the

fieldmouse. 'I wish some of the other mice could see me now.' And he gave a loud squeak.

Sure enough, another fieldmouse heard him, and when he saw the fine-looking ship he called the other mice, and in the end there were eight little fieldmice sailing along on the hat. The one who got on first was the captain, the second was his mate and the rest were the crew.

You have no idea what fun those fieldmice had with Mr. Puffblow's hat that autumn! Every day they went for a sail, and when winter came and it got too cold, they dragged the hat on to dry land and used it for a house. All through the winter they sat inside it, snug and warm, telling each other mouse fairy-tales and singing mouse carols at Christmas.

And when spring came they started sailing again.

Then one day there was a great noise and to-do in the wood. A whole crowd of children from the town were out for a picnic. There was a man with them and they were all laughing and shouting and having a fine time together. The man carried the smallest one on his shoulders while the others were clinging to his coat-tails. They picked flowers for him and showed him all the nicest things they could find in the wood on a spring day.

Suddenly they stopped by the brook. 'Look over there!' cried one of the children. 'Look at that big hat on the other bank!'

The mice had just dragged the hat out of the brook because they were going home to supper.

When the man saw the hat he laughed and laughed. Because, you see, he knew it.

Can you guess who he was? Mr. Puffblow! But a very much nicer Mr. Puffblow now, and do you know why? Well, when he used to wear that enormous hat on his head he was always afraid the children would laugh at him. But from the moment he lost the hat he became quite different; he was no longer afraid.

'There's your old hat, Mr. Puffblow!' shouted the children with glee. 'Don't you want to wear it again?'

'Certainly not!' said Mr. Puffblow. 'Come along now, children, let's pick anemones.'

So they did.

And the fieldmice are using Mr. Puffblow's hat for a ship to this day.

Miriam-from-America

THERE was once a doll who was so beautifully smart that she had to sit all day, every day, on top of a chest of drawers. She couldn't *do* anything, not even shut her eyes or stand on her feet, and her fine silk dress was sewn on to her body, so she couldn't be undressed. But there was no doubt about it; she was the grandest of all the dolls just because she sat on top of the chest of drawers.

The little girl who owned the doll never allowed her school friends to touch her. When they asked why they mustn't touch her, the little girl said:

'Don't you know that this doll is called Miriam and comes from America? What's more, she's crossed the Atlantic in a ship, and even *I'm* not allowed to touch her till I'm a big girl.'

When her friends heard this their eyes grew round with astonishment and, putting their hands behind their backs, they stood and stared at Miriam-from-America.

One day the window near the chest of drawers stood

open, and someone opened the door as well so that there was a draught. This blew Miriam off the chest straight out of the window into the garden below. There she lay, quite still, looking up at the sky.

It grew darker and darker, until it was late night and the stars began to twinkle. All at once, the full moon came sailing across the sky.

'What is that strange-looking thing in the garden?' said the moon, and turned his light on Miriam.

Miriam said nothing; she just went on lying there. But the wind whistled in the tree tops and answered for her: 'That is Miriam-from-America. She is the most elegant doll because she usually sits right on top of a chest of drawers.'

'Can't she speak for herself?' asked the moon.

'I don't think so,' said the wind. 'Can you talk, Miriam?'

Miriam said nothing.

'Try and talk to us—just a little,' said the moon.

Miriam still didn't move, but the moon saw she wanted to say something, so he waited.

'Over the sea and under the sky!' Miriam said suddenly.

'Why do you say "over the sea and under the sky"?' asked the moon.

'Because I have sailed over the sea,' said Miriam, 'and I thought that was great fun. And now I'm lying under the sky and that is even more fun.'

'But I suppose sitting on a chest of drawers being the most elegant, the most beautiful, doll is more fun still?' said the wind.

'It's the dullest thing in the world!' said Miriam. 'Couldn't you two help me so that I don't have to be so elegant, so smart, any more?'

'That's easy,' said the wind, and blew Miriam straight into a big puddle. Miriam laughed; it was lovely to splash about in water. She had never tried that before.

'I must help too,' said the moon, and he threw a beam of light on the kennel where the dog Rover lay asleep. He woke up at once and saw Miriam lying in the puddle. So he took her smart silk dress between his

teeth and ran down the road with her. Miriam was jolted up and down, but she didn't mind a bit because she knew Rover well; she had often seen him from her chest of drawers when he lay curled up by the fire. And now here she was, having a lovely game with him!

The moon followed them down the street, and so did the wind, turning somersaults all the way. At last they came back to the house where Miriam lived. But how was she to get indoors again? The window was still open but Miriam couldn't possibly climb up to it.

'We shall have to ask the crow to carry her up in his beak,' said the moon. So they did. The crow was very ready to help. He flew through the window with Miriam and set her down on the chest of drawers.

Well, you can imagine the fuss there was next day when the little girl's mother saw what a mess Miriam was in! But the little girl was very pleased, because from now on she could play with Miriam as much as she liked. She took her for rides in the doll's pram, and every time the wind blew Miriam waved her hand—just a little bit. This was supposed to mean:

'Thank you, wind, for helping me get away from the chest of drawers!'

Jumping Jack and his friends

THE things I am going to tell you about in this story only happened last night. They happened after everyone had gone to bed; not only the little children and the big children, but the grown-ups as well.

In a shed—an ordinary kind of garden shed which people use for bicycles and shovels and rakes and spades —lived a family of toys.

There was a tricycle, a skipping rope hanging on a nail and two hop-scotch stones stuck in a crack in the floor. Almost hidden, stood a little red wheelbarrow which the children used in the sand pit, and in it lay a ball and a jumping jack. This jumping jack was so smart he had his name painted across his back in big letters: JUMPING JACK.

The toys had been in the shed all winter. They had seen the snowdrifts when the grown-ups came for shovels to clear the paths, and they had heard the wind howl and sigh. But just lately the toys had heard a new noise—a slow *drip* . . . *drip* . . . from the roof. Then it had turned into *drippy-drippy-drop* and at last a very quick *drip*,

drip, drip, drip, and they knew that all the snow had melted from the roof.

'Are we going out now?' asked Jumping Jack, who had never seen winter before.

'Not for a long time yet,' answered the Wheelbarrow.

One day a little boy came for the Tricycle. He got on it and pedalled out into the spring sunshine, ringing his bell loudly.

'Will it be our turn next?' asked Jumping Jack.

'Not yet,' said the Wheelbarrow.

Then a little girl, whose name was Cathy, came into the shed. 'Look, there's my ball!' she shouted, and hugged the Ball tightly. But it sagged and made a hissing noise because it had a split in its rubber tummy.

'Oh, you horrid Ball!' Cathy cried, and threw it back in the Wheelbarrow. Instead she took the Skipping Rope and ran out with it into the sunshine. She jumped and skipped so hard her hair stood out like a halo round her head.

'Why didn't she take the Ball with her?' asked Jumping Jack. But the Wheelbarrow only said 'Hmm.' It didn't want to be unkind to the poor Ball.

Nothing more was said. But a few days later they could hear a bouncing noise outside the shed; *bump-bump* it went against the wall, and the Wheelbarrow knew what that meant. So did the Old Ball; it lay there sighing through its crack all day long.

The Wheelbarrow thought about this for a long time —several days and nights. Then last night, after everyone had gone to bed, as I said, it gave a wooden creak and said to the Old Ball:

'I think it's a shame you're never to go out in the sunshine again. And I'm sorry to have to be the one to tell you, but you do understand, don't you, that Cathy has got a new ball and she's forgotten about you?'

'Yes,' sighed the Old Ball.

'I don't think Peter has forgotten *me*,' said Jumping Jack; 'he made such a fuss of me last summer. Anyway, it was just a mistake my being put out here in the shed. It was the charlady who carried all the summer toys out here when the snow came, and she didn't notice I'd got mixed up with them. I've been jumping mad ever since!'

'There's no need to get hoity-toity and stick your nose in the air even if you were only made last summer. You never know how long you will last. I've seen many jumping jacks in my time. They're fine as long as the strings don't break and both arms and legs are working. But sooner or later something gets broken and that's the end of that. . . . Well, not always, of course!' he added quickly when he saw that Jumping Jack looked quite frightened and ready to cry.

'I'm not at all perfect myself,' the Wheelbarrow went on. 'There's a weakness in one of my arms. The carpenter, who made me, put a thick layer of paint over the crack, so that it wouldn't show. But I've often been afraid when Peter filled me up with sand. Last year, I almost broke several times, so I don't think he'll use me again when summer comes along.'

'What a shame!' wheezed the Old Ball. He was sorry for the Wheelbarrow, but pleased at the same time that he wouldn't be left all alone in the dark shed.

'Then it's just me who is going out in the sunshine,' said Jumping Jack in a cheeky sort of way.

'You ought to be ashamed of yourself!' said the Wheelbarrow. 'We're all in the same boat—or rather, you and the Old Ball are in the same barrow, and that barrow happens to be me. And now I'm going to tell you what we're going to do—we three.'

'Do? What can we three do?' asked Jumping Jack.

'Listen. A long time ago there was an old wheelbarrow in here which told me that a night would come
when all old broken or unwanted toys would come to
life and go off and find new homes for themselves. I've
been waiting for that night ever since, and now tonight
I really think it's come, for I feel a sort of twitching and
tingling in my wheel as if it wants to run. Yes, I'm sure
we must be off!'

'But I don't want to go with you!' shouted Jumping
Jack, 'I want to stay with Peter. I want to go back to the
nursery with all the other toys; I don't want to go to a
new home!'

But before he could say any more the Wheelbarrow

lifted his arms and rolled out of the shed with the Old
Ball and Jumping Jack. The wheel creaked, the Old Ball
sighed and Jumping Jack's arms and legs were tossing to
and fro, so that it looked as if he was trying to get out,
which, of course, was what he *wanted* to do. But the
Wheelbarrow just went steadily on, balancing on one
wheel.

Soon they met other toys; first a tricycle with crooked

handlebars which lurched from one side of the road to the other and nearly ran over them.

'Good evening,' said the Wheelbarrow.

'I think you should say "Good night" when it's so late,' said the Tricycle. 'I don't know why, but I had such an awful itch in my pedals, I just had to come out on to the road. And now I don't know where I'm going. . . .' And he was off, lurching from side to side.

After a while they met a doll with only one arm.

'Good night!' said the Wheelbarrow, for he was not going to make the same mistake twice.

'Good night!' said the Doll as she danced and pranced in her pink knitted slippers.

'Where are you going?' the Wheelbarrow called after her.

'I don't know. And I don't know where I come from. I just know I have to keep on and on!'

'Why couldn't she have come with us?' asked Jumping Jack, when she had disappeared.

'Stupid!' said the Barrow. 'Don't you understand that the whole idea is that each toy should go to a different home? If one child gets a whole lot of old broken toys the same thing will happen again—some of them will be thrown away. No, each child is to have *one* toy.' And they rolled on.

They met many queer toys.

A skipping rope came waving along the road, and after it a humming-top, tripping and bumping over the stones in the road. A very small toy train came chuffing along at full speed. It headed straight for the ditch and disappeared under the water. But a moment later—*bubble-bubble, bubble-bubble, whoosh!*—up it came on the other side and ran straight into a wooden hoop which was bowling in the opposite direction. The hoop fell over, the train fell over, but that didn't worry them; they were up and off again before you could count three. A teddy-bear with a split down the back came plodding by. All he needed was a bit more sawdust stuffing and a few stitches, and some little girl would be glad to have him and mend his back.

After a time the Old Ball started rolling about in the barrow in a restless sort of way: 'I say, Wheelbarrow, can you stop a minute? There's a little cottage up there by the wood; something tells me I have to get off here.'

The Wheelbarrow stopped to let the Old Ball roll off, and it bounced up on the cottage window to look in. Sure enough there was a little girl asleep in bed clutching an old rag doll.

'This must be the place all right,' said the Old Ball. 'Thanks for bringing me along and for being so kind to me. I'll just stay here on the doorstep, then she's sure to find me in the morning. Goodbye!'

The Wheelbarrow and Jumping Jack said goodbye and rolled on until the Barrow suddenly said, 'I can feel a sort of pull inside me; I think we have to turn up this little path through the wood.'

So they did. There was still a bit of snow here and there, making the wheel go *crunch, crunch*.

At last they came to a clearing with an even smaller

cottage than the one where the Old Ball had stopped.
The snow lay in drifts against the windows, so the Wheelbarrow took a run at one of them and managed to get
high enough to look in. And there was a little boy asleep.
By the stove stood a box with a string tied to it. That was
all *he* had in the way of a wheelbarrow.

'There, I *thought* so!' said the Wheelbarrow. 'This is the
place for me. But what about you, Jack? Haven't *you* felt
anything yet? Haven't you had an itch in those long arms
and legs of yours as if somebody was pulling your string?'

'No, I haven't!' said Jumping Jack very crossly. 'I'm

not broken, that's why. It's only the broken and cast-off toys who have to find new homes; I have Peter to love me at home, and I don't know why you brought me along—especially when I shouted to you to let me off, you stupid old bundle of sticks!'

'It wasn't my fault. Just when you wanted to get out, something told me to start off and take you with me, so I did.'

Then suddenly the Barrow *knew* why he had brought Jack along. 'Don't you understand? You had to see for yourself what happens tonight, so that you can go home and tell all the other toys. You must tell them they needn't worry even if they do get broken. There are lots of children who will have them and mend them too, so that they're as good as new.'

And all at once Jumping Jack could see it too. 'You're quite right,' he said.

And then he found, to his surprise, that he could move. What fun it was to stretch his legs and arms without being jerked by the string! He hopped first on one leg, then the other, and then he turned complete somersaults. Then he thanked the Wheelbarrow for his trip and said goodbye.

After that, with his string floating straight out behind him like a tail, he ran and ran till he reached the little shed in the garden at home.

And now Jumping Jack has been waiting all day for it to grow dark; for not until the children are in bed and asleep can he go out and give his message to all the broken and unwanted toys.

*   *   *   *   *

So if you wake up tomorrow morning and find that your old doll seems to be smiling just a little, or that your chipped trumpet sounds better than it has for a long time, that will be because Jumping Jack has told them about the trip he made with his friends the Wheelbarrow and the Old Ball last night.

The potato with big ideas

THERE was once a potato which lay waiting for someone to come and dig it up. The other potatoes were just

quietly growing larger and larger, but this particular potato had ideas; he was stuck-up. And he was bored with waiting.

'Hi, everybody!' the stuck-up potato said. 'I'm not

going to wait any longer. I'll try to get out of this hole by myself. People must be longing to see what a beautiful potato I am; everything that is beautiful must see the light of day and enjoy the sunshine. Here I come! The most beautiful potato in all the world!'

You may know that all potatoes are tied to the mother potato by a thin thread (so that she can keep them in order, no doubt). Now that stuck-up potato began tugging at his thread, and the thread stretched and stretched till one fine day the stuck-up potato found himself lying on the ground above.

'Hurrah, hurrah! Here I am at last! Good morning, Mr. Weed! Good morning, Mrs. Worm! I am the world's most beautiful potato. And if you, Mr. Sun, would like to shine on me for a moment, you can.'

'With the greatest of pleasure,' answered the sun, 'but it won't be good for you, you know.'

'Who cares? You just shine away and let me enjoy a nice hot sun-bath.'

So the sun shone on that stuck-up potato and turned him blue, green, red and purple all over. This made the potato more pleased with himself than ever:

'When the boys come past and see me lying here they will say: "My goodness! What a fine potato! We must take that home to Mother for dinner." And one of them will put me carefully in his pocket. When his mother sees me she will say: "Goodness gracious! What a wonderful potato; it's much too good for me. I will give it to the parson." And when the parson sees me he will say: "Goodness gracious! My, oh my! What a marvellous potato; I'll give it to the bishop." And when the bishop sees me he will say: "Goodness gracious! My, oh my! And bless my soul! But what an exquisite potato. I must send it straight to the Pope in Rome." Then I will be wrapped in silver paper and sent to the Pope. And when the Pope sees me he will put on his finest clothes and sit on his best silver throne and put me on a gold plate and eat me, while all the church bells ring to tell the world that now the Pope is eating the most beautiful potato from Puddlington-on-the-Marsh.'

But just as the potato was having this lovely dream, the farmer and his wife and their little boy came out into the field to start lifting the potatoes.

They sang as they worked, and shouted to each other every time they found a really whacking big potato.

'Wait till they see *me*, then they'll have something to crow about!' thought the stuck-up potato.

Suddenly the little boy shouted: 'Look at this funny-looking potato! It's blue and red and green all over!'

'Throw it in the pig-bucket,' said his father; 'you can't eat that sort. It's been on top of the earth instead of underneath, where it should have been. But the pigs won't mind what colour it is.'

And so that stuck-up potato ended his days in the pig-trough instead of on a gold plate in the Pope's palace in Rome, which all goes to show that even if you have big ideas it's sometimes wiser to leave them alone.

The mice and the Christmas tree

Now you shall hear the story about a family of mice who lived behind the larder wall.

*   *   *   *   *

Every Christmas Eve, Mother Mouse and the children swept and dusted their whole house with their tails, and for a Christmas tree Father Mouse decorated an old boot with spider's web instead of tinsel. For Christmas presents, the children were each given a little nut, and Mother Mouse held up a piece of bacon fat for them all to sniff.

After that, they danced round and round the boot, and sang and played games till they were tired out. Then

Father Mouse would say: 'That's all for tonight! Time to go to bed!'

That is how it had been every Christmas and that is how it was to be this year. The little mice held each other by the tail and danced round the boot, while Granny Mouse enjoyed the fun from her rocking-chair, which wasn't a rocking-chair at all, but a small turnip.

But when Father Mouse said, 'That's all for tonight! Time to go to bed!' all the children dropped each other's tails and shouted: 'No! No!'

'What's that?' said Father Mouse. 'When I say it's time for bed, it's time for bed!'

'We don't want to go!' cried the children, and hid behind Granny's turnip rocking-chair.

'What's all this nonsense?' said Mother Mouse. 'Christmas is over now, so off you go, the lot of you!'

'No, no!' wailed the children, and climbed on to Granny's knee. She hugged them all lovingly. 'Why don't you want to go to bed, my little sugar lumps?'

'Because we want to go upstairs to the big drawing-

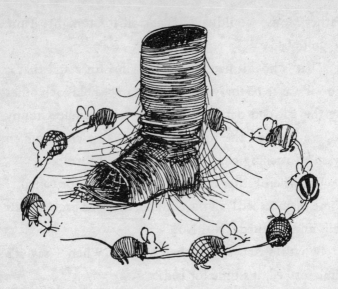

room and dance round a proper Christmas tree,' said the eldest Mouse child. 'You see, I've been peeping through a crack in the wall and I saw a huge Christmas tree with lots and lots of lights on it.'

'We want to see the Christmas tree and all the lights too!' shouted the other children.

'Oh, but the drawing-room can be a very dangerous place for mice,' said Granny.

'Not when all the people have gone to bed,' objected the eldest Mouse child.

'Oh, do let's go!' they all pleaded.

Mother and Father Mouse didn't know what to say, but they couldn't very well disappoint the children on Christmas Eve.

'Perhaps we could take them up there just for a minute or two,' suggested Mother Mouse.

'Very well,' said Father, 'but follow me closely.'

So they set off. They tiptoed past three tins of herring, two large jars of honey and a barrel of cider.

'We have to go very carefully here,' whispered Father Mouse, 'not to knock over any bottles. Are you all right, Granny?'

'Of course I'm all right,' said Granny, 'you just carry on. I haven't been up in the drawing-room since I was a little Mouse girl; it'll be fun to see it all again.'

'Mind the trap!' said the eldest Mouse child. 'It's behind that sack of potatoes.'

'I know that,' said Granny; 'it's been there since I was

a child. I'm not afraid of that!' And she took a flying leap right over the trap and scuttled after the others up the wall.

'What a lovely tree!' cried all the children when they peeped out of the hole by the drawing-room fireplace. 'But where are the lights? You said there'd be lots and lots of lights, didn't you? Didn't you?' The children shouted, crowding round the eldest one, who was quite sure there had been lights the day before.

They stood looking for a little while. Then suddenly a whole lot of coloured lights lit up the tree! Do you know what had happened? By accident, Granny had touched the electric switch by the fireplace.

'Oh, how lovely!' they all exclaimed, and Father and Mother and Granny thought it was very nice too. They walked right round the tree, looking at the decorations, the little paper baskets, the glass balls and the glittering tinsel garlands. But the children found something even more exciting: a mechanical lorry!

Of course, they couldn't wind it up themselves, but its young master had wound it up before he went to bed, to be ready for him to play with in the morning. So when the Mouse children clambered into it, it started off right away.

'Children, children! You mustn't make such a noise!' warned Mother Mouse.

But the children didn't listen; they were having a wonderful time going round and round and round in the lorry.

'As long as the cat doesn't come!' said Father Mouse anxiously.

He had hardly spoken before the cat walked silently through the open door.

Father, Mother and Granny Mouse all made a dash for the hole in the skirting but the children were trapped in the lorry, which just went on going round and round and round. They had never been so scared in all their Mouse lives.

The cat crouched under the tree, and every time the lorry passed she tried to tap it with her front paw. But it was going too fast and she missed.

Then the lorry started slowing down. 'I think we'd better make a jump for it and try to get up in the tree,' said the eldest Mouse. So when the lorry stopped they all gave a big jump and landed on the branches of the tree.

One hid in a paper basket, another behind a bulb (which nearly burned him), a third swung on a glass ball and the fourth rolled himself up in some cotton wool. But where was the eldest Mouse? Oh yes, he had climbed right to the top and was balancing next to the star and shouting at the cat:

'Silly, silly cat,
You can't catch us!
You're much too fat,
Silly, silly cat!'

But the cat pretended not to hear or see the little mice. She sharpened her claws on the lorry. 'I'm not interested in catching mice tonight,' she said as if to herself, 'I've been waiting for a chance to play with this lorry all day.'

'Pooh! That's just a story!' said the eldest who was also the bravest. 'You'd catch us quick enough if we came down.'

'No, I wouldn't. Not on Christmas Eve!' said the cat. And she kept her word. When they did all come timidly down, she never moved, but just said: 'Hurry back to your hole, children. Christmas Eve is the one night when I'm kind to little mice. But woe betide you if I catch you tomorrow morning!'

The little mice pelted through that hole and never stopped running till they got to their home behind the larder wall. There were Father and Mother and Granny Mouse waiting in fear and trembling to know what had happened to them.

When Mother Mouse had heard their story she said, 'You must promise me, children, never to go up to the drawing-room again.'

'We promise! We promise!' they all shouted together.
Then she made them say after her *The Mouse Law*, which
they'd all been taught when they were tiny:

'We promise always to obey
Our parents dear in every way,
To wipe our feet upon the mat
And never, never cheek the cat.

Remember too the awful danger
Of taking money from a stranger;
We will not go off on our own
Or give our mother cause to moan.

Odd bits of cheese and bacon-scraps
Are almost certain to be traps,
So we must look for bigger things
Like loaves and cakes and doughnut-rings;

And if these rules we still obey
We'll live to run another day.'

Never take no for an answer

You see the old woman spinning yarn? She was hard at work one day when a young mouse came out of the hole by the stove.

'Well, well, fancy seeing you,' said the old woman.

'Peep, peep!' said the little mouse. 'My ma sent me to ask what the yarn is for that you're spinning?'

'It's for a jersey for my husband; the one he has is so worn he can't use it any more,' answered the old woman.

'Peep, peep! I'd better go and tell that to my ma!' And the little mouse disappeared down the hole. The old woman went on spinning, but it wasn't long before she heard a scuffling by the stove and there sat the mouse once more.

'You back again?' she asked.

'Peep, peep! My ma said to ask you who is to have your husband's old jersey when he gets the new one?'

'I'm going to use that myself when I milk the cows, because my old milking jacket isn't fit to wear any more,' said the old woman.

'Peep, peep! I'd better go and tell that to my ma,' said the mouse, and he was gone. But in no time at all he was back again.

'What d'you want to know this time?' the old woman asked.

'Peep, peep! My ma wants to know who is to have your old milking jacket when you get your husband's old jersey and he gets the new one?'

'The dog is going to have it in his kennel, because his old rug is so thin it's no good any more.'

'Peep, peep! I'd better go and tell that to my ma,' said the little mouse, and darted away to his hole by the stove. But he had hardly popped in before he popped out again.

'That was quick!' said the woman. 'What is it now?'

'Peep, peep! My ma wants to know who is to have the dog's old rug when he gets your old milking jacket and you get your husband's old jersey and he gets the new one?' said the mouse all in one breath.

'You can have it, if you like,' said the old woman.

'Peep, peep! Thank you *very* much,' said the little mouse. 'Now there'll be an eiderdown for *our* bed as well!' And he was so pleased he sang this song:

> 'Oh me, oh my!
> We'll soon be as snug
> As a bug in a rug,
> What do you think of that!
> Come and see me any time
> I'll make you up another rhyme,
> But please don't bring the cat.'

Mr. Learn-a-lot and the singing midges

ONE warm summer night Mrs. Midge said to her daughters, 'We'll go and visit Mr. Learn-a-lot, the schoolmaster.'

'What do we want to do that for?' asked the young midges. There were three of them: Big Sister Midge, Middle Sister Midge and Wee Sister Midge.

'We're going to sing to him. You're all so good at singing now, it's a pleasure to listen to you, and Mr. Learn-a-lot is such a good judge of music.'

So they all flew off to Mr. Learn-a-lot's house and hovered outside his bedroom window. Mrs. Midge peered through the glass while her daughters all talked at once in high, squeaky voices:

'Is the window shut, Mama?'

'Won't he open it, Mama?'

'Can't we get in, Mama?'

'I expect he'll open the window when he goes to bed,' said Mrs. Midge.

'He's opening the window now, Mama!'

'Can we go in now, Mama?'

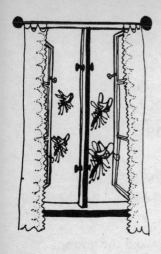

'What shall we sing for him, Mama?'

'Not so fast, children, there's no hurry. Let Mr. Learn-a-lot get nicely into bed first.'

'He's climbing into bed now, Mama! He's in bed, really he is, Mama! Wouldn't it be dreadful if he fell asleep before he heard our singing, Mama?' squeaked all the little midges. But Mrs. Midge was sure the school-master would wake up again when they started singing.

'I think Big Sister Midge had better go in first,' she said.

'All right, but what am I to sing, Mama?'

'You can sing the song about "We midges have not got . . .",' said Mrs. Midge, and settled herself with her two younger daughters behind the curtain. 'And remember to fly in a circle over his head. If he likes your song he will sit up in bed. Now off you go!'

And Big Sister Midge flew round and round in a circle over Mr. Learn-a-lot's head and sang this song:

> 'We midges have not got a couple of beans
> Yet in summer we all are as happy as queens,
> For every night in a swoon of delight
> We dance to the tune of our dizzy flight,
> And all we need to keep in the pink
> Is a tiny drop of your blood to drink.'

Three times she sang the same verse, and she was beginning to think Mr. Learn-a-lot didn't care for her song at all. But suddenly he sat bolt upright in bed.

'Come back! Come back, child!' whispered Mrs. Midge.

'Was I all right, Mama?'

'You were very good. Now we'll just wait till Mr. Learn-a-lot has fallen asleep again, then it'll be Middle Sister's turn. You can sing the song about "How doth the little busy me"—that is so very funny! There! Now I think it would be all right for you to start. But you mustn't leave off before Mr. Learn-a-lot has got right out of bed and is standing in the middle of the floor. Fly a little higher than your sister did. Off you go!'

And Middle Sister Midge sang as loudly as she could while she flew round and round the schoolmaster's head:

> 'How doth the little busy me
> Improve each shady hour
> By settling on your nose or knee
> As if upon a flower.'

She hadn't sung more than one verse before Mr. Learn-a-lot threw off the bedclothes and tumbled out of bed.

'Come back, come back!' whispered Mrs. Midge.

'Wasn't I good?' said Middle Sister as she arrived back all out of breath. 'And I wasn't a bit afraid of him!'

'That'll do; we midges are not in the habit of boasting,' said Mrs. Midge. 'Now it's Wee Sister's turn.'

'What shall I sing?' asked the smallest midge with the tiniest voice you ever heard.

'You can sing our evening song—you know—the one that goes:

> 'The day is done and all rejoice
> To hear again this still small voice.
> May the music of my wings
> Console you for my little stings.'

That's just the thing for tonight,' Mrs. Midge added thoughtfully.

'Oh yes, I know that one,' said Wee Sister; she was very pleased her mother had chosen one she knew.

'I expect it will be the last song tonight,' said Mrs. Midge, 'and don't worry if you don't get right through it. If Mr. Learn-a-lot suddenly claps his hands you must be sure to come back to me at once. Will you remember that?'

'Yes, Mama,' said Wee Sister, and off she flew.

Mr. Learn-a-lot was lying absolutely still. So Wee Sister began to sing—all on one top note:

'The day is done——'

Smack! Mr. Learn-a-lot clapped his hands together.

'Come back, come back!' called Mrs. Midge. But there was no sign of Wee Sister.

'Oh, my darling, sweet wee one, please come back to your mother!' wailed Mrs. Midge. No sound—no sound at all for a long time; then suddenly Wee Sister was sitting on the curtain beside them.

'Didn't you hear me calling?' asked Mrs. Midge very sternly.

'Oh yes, but you said I was to fly very, very quietly, and that clap of Mr. Learn-a-lot's sent me flying right into the darkest corner of the room.'

'Poor darling!' said Mrs. Midge. 'But you're safe back now. You've all been very good and very clever girls. And now I'd like to hear what you think of Mr. Learn-a-lot?'

Big Sister answered, 'He's nice; he likes the one who sings longest best!'

Middle Sister answered, 'He's very polite; he gets out of bed for the one who sings loudest!'

And Wee Sister said, 'I think he's very musical; he claps the one with the sweetest voice!'

'Yes, yes, that's all very true,' said Mrs. Midge; 'but now I will tell you something else about Mr. Learn-a-lot. He is not only a very learned gentleman, but he will provide us with the nicest, most enjoyable supper, and we needn't even wake him up. Shall we go?'

'Oh, that is a fine idea!' cried Big Sister, Middle Sister and Wee Sister Midge, for they always did just what their mother told them.

Poor Mr. Learn-a-lot!

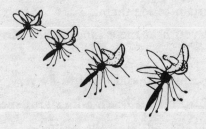